Poké Rap!

I want to be the very best there ever was
To beat all the rest, yeah, that's my cause

Catch 'em, Catch 'em, Gotta catch 'em all

Pokémon I'll search across the land
Look far and wide
Release from my hand
The power that's inside

Catch 'em, Catch 'em, Gotta catch 'em all Pokémon!

Gotta catch 'em all, Gotta catch 'em all
Gotta catch 'em all, Gotta catch 'em all

At least one hundred and fifty or more to see
To be a Pokémon Master is my destiny

Catch 'em, Catch 'em, Gotta catch 'em all
Gotta catch 'em all, Pokémon! (repeat three times)

Can YOU Rap all 150?

Here's the first 32 Pokémon.
Catch the next book *Ash Ketchum, Pokémon Detective*
for more of the Poké Rap.

Electrode, Diglett, Nidoran, Mankey
Venusaur, Rattata, Fearow, Pidgey
Seaking, Jolteon, Dragonite, Gastly
Ponyta, Vaporeon, Poliwrath, Butterfree

Venomoth, Poliwag, Nidorino, Golduck
Ivysaur, Grimer, Victreebel, Moltres
Nidoking, Farfetch'd, Abra, Jigglypuff
Kingler, Rhyhorn, Clefable, Wigglytuff

Words and Music by Tamara Loeffler and John Siegler
Copyright © 1999 Pikachu Music (BMI)
Worldwide rights for Pikachu Music administered by Cherry River Music Co. (BMI)
All Rights Reserved   Used by Permission

Collect them all!

Go West, Young Ash

The publisher does not have any control over and does not assume any responsibility for author or third-party websites or their content.

No part of this publication may be reproduced, stored in a retrieval system, or transmitted in any form or by any means, electronic, mechanical, photocopying, recording, or otherwise, without written permission of the publisher. For information regarding permission, write to Scholastic Inc., Attention: Permissions Department, 557 Broadway, New York, NY 10012.

This book is a work of fiction. Names, characters, places, and incidents are either the product of the author's imagination or are used fictitiously, and any resemblance to actual persons, living or dead, business establishments, events, or locales is entirely coincidental.

ISBN 978-1-338-28402-7

10 9 8 7 6 5 4 3 2   18 19 20 21 22

Printed in the U.S.A.   40
First printing 2018

Go West, Young Ash

Adapted by Tracey West

Scholastic Inc.

Pikachu vs. Eevee

"Ash! It's good to see you," Professor Oak said.

Ash Ketchum walked into Professor Oak's lab and smiled. Professor Oak hadn't changed a bit since the last time Ash had seen him. He still wore a white lab coat. Ash figured Professor Oak was too busy studying Pokémon to worry about how he looked.

"It's good to see you, too, Professor," Ash said.

Professor Oak knelt down and patted the little yellow Pokémon at Ash's side. "You're certainly looking well, Pikachu," Professor Oak said.

"*Pika!*" Pikachu replied happily.

Ash's three friends walked into the lab behind him.

Misty, a Pokémon Trainer, had an energetic personality that matched her bright orange hair. She carried Togepi, a tiny Pokémon, in her arms.

Brock was studying to become a Pokémon breeder. His eyes glanced around the lab from under his mop of spiky dark hair. Brock had just met up with Ash and Misty after taking time off to study with a famous Pokémon breeder, Professor Ivy.

Tracey was a new friend Ash and Misty had met on their journey to the Orange Islands. He was a Pokémon watcher who studied Pokémon behavior and drew pictures of them. Professor Oak was Tracey's hero.

"It's such an honor to finally meet you," Tracey said, pumping Professor Oak's hand. "I have some reports of my studies that I'd love to show you. It would mean so much to me."

"I'd be happy to — later," Professor Oak said. "Right now, I'm anxious to get the GS Ball from Ash."

"Right," Ash said. The reason Ash had traveled to the Orange Islands was to bring the mysterious Poké Ball to Professor Oak. It couldn't be transported from one lab to another like most regular Poké Balls. Most Poké Balls were red and white and held captured Pokémon. The GS Ball was gold and silver. No one could figure out how to open it or what was inside.

Ash reached into his backpack and retrieved the shiny ball. He handed it to the professor.

Professor Oak studied the ball, a pleased smile on his face. "Marvelous! Good work, Ash."

Ash beamed. Professor Oak had started Ash on his Pokémon journey by giving him Pikachu, his very first Pokémon. Ash wanted to make Professor Oak proud. He had made many mistakes on his journey. He had a lot to learn if he was ever going to become a Pokémon Master.

Bringing the GS Ball to Professor Oak felt good.

"Well, if it isn't that loser, Ash Ketchum," a nasal voice twanged.

Ash knew that voice. It was Gary, Professor Oak's grandson, and Ash's biggest rival.

"Who are you calling a loser?" Ash asked. He and Gary faced each other, nose to nose. Gary reached for a Poké Ball.

"Not in the lab!" Professor Oak said, stepping between them to stop the battle. "Let's all go outside."

"Gary stopped by for a visit," Professor Oak said as the others followed him to the green lawn outside the lab. "He wanted to surprise you."

"Some surprise," Ash said under his breath. He turned to Gary. "I'm no loser. I won the Orange Islands Winner's Cup, you know."

"Big deal," Gary said. "I'm still better than you."

"Oh, yeah?" Ash asked.

"These guys argue more than Ash and Misty," Tracey remarked.

Ash looked Gary in the eye. "Let's settle this once and for all."

"You're on!" Gary said. "Let's battle with our best Pokémon. One-on-one."

A cool spring breeze kicked up, blowing strands of dark hair into Ash's face. He pulled down his red-and-white cap and stared at Gary. He had to concentrate. He had to win.

Pikachu stood next to Ash. The lightning mouse wore a look of determination on its face.

"My Pokémon will be Pikachu," Ash said.

"Pika!" said Pikachu.

"I see," Gary said. "In that case, I choose Eevee!"

Gary threw out a red-and-white Poké Ball. A cute, furry Pokémon appeared. Eevee had a bushy tail, pointy ears, and big, dark eyes.

"How adorable," Misty cooed.

"That's not all it is," Brock said. "That Eevee is in great shape. I'll bet its powers are tough to beat."

"I've heard most Trainers use special stones to evolve Eevee into Flareon, Jolteon, or Vaporeon," Tracey added.

Brock stepped onto the grass, halfway between Ash and Gary.

"You two need a judge for this match," Brock said. He cleared his throat, then yelled, "Pikachu versus Eevee. This will be a one-on-one battle, with no time limit!"

Ash didn't waste any time. "Pikachu, Quick Attack!"

Pikachu ran across the field so fast it looked like a yellow blur.

Gary acted quickly, too. "Eevee, Reflect!"

At Gary's command, a clear, protective bubble formed around Eevee. Pikachu slammed into the bubble. The bubble burst, and Pikachu bounced backward. Eevee was thrown into the air, but the Pokémon landed safely on its feet.

"That Reflect attack was a lot stronger than usual," Tracey remarked, impressed.

"What do you mean?" asked Misty.

"Usually Reflect can only keep a Pokémon safe from about half of the damage in an attack," Tracey explained. "But Eevee didn't seem to suffer any damage at all."

"Wow," Misty said. "Gary's Eevee must be strong!"

Ash knew he had to choose another attack.

"Pikachu, Thunderbolt!" Ash cried.

Pikachu prepared for the move. Its red cheeks sizzled with electric sparks.

"Eevee, Double Team!" Gary called out.

Ash watched, curious to see what the attack was about. Eevee glowed with white light.

Then, in a flash, six more Eevee appeared on the field!

"Hit them all, Pikachu," Ash said.

Pikachu hurled an electric blast at the first Eevee in line. The Eevee vanished in a blaze of light.

The next Eevee was hit. Zap! That Eevee disappeared into thin air, too.

Suddenly, Ash realized what the attack was about.

"They're illusions, Pikachu!" Ash yelled. "We've got to find the real Eevee!"

2

A New Journey

Startled, Pikachu hesitated.

Gary quickly took advantage. "Eevee, Take Down!"

The Eevee illusions disappeared. The real Eevee stood alone on the field. It ran at Pikachu with all its might.

"Get out of there, Pikachu," Ash said. "Use your Agility!"

Pikachu expertly dodged Eevee's Take Down attack, darting from one part of the field to another. Eevee didn't know which way to turn.

"All right!" Ash said. "Now try Thunder."

Little white lightning bolts sparked from Pikachu's

body. Pikachu built up energy, ready to hurl it at Eevee.

"Eevee, Skull Bash!" Gary cried.

Eevee leaped into the air. A force field of white-hot energy encircled its body.

Pikachu jumped up at the same time, ready to deliver a powerful Thunder attack.

Pikachu didn't have a chance. Eevee collided with Pikachu. The energy field sent Pikachu soaring into the air. The electricity from the Thunder attack exploded like a firecracker. Pikachu slammed back down into the ground.

Pikachu struggled to get up. But the little yellow Pokémon just couldn't do it. Pikachu collapsed in an exhausted heap.

"The match is decided. Eevee wins!" Brock shouted.

Eevee joyfully ran over to Gary.

"Good work, Eevee!" Gary said. He petted Eevee's furry brown head. Then he held out a Poké Ball, and Eevee disappeared inside.

Ash hugged Pikachu. "You did your best, Pikachu. Thanks! We'll beat Gary next time."

"Pika pi," Pikachu said, giving Ash a weak smile.

Ash was glad Pikachu was all right. Getting beaten by Gary hurt, but he'd always have another chance.

And there was no shame in losing to Eevee. Ash had rarely seen a Pokémon with so much skill.

They went back into the lab and before long, the sun began to set.

"Hey, Professor Oak, where's Gary?" Ash asked. He was ready for a rematch.

But Professor Oak didn't answer. He and the others were intently studying the GS Ball. The professor had the ball hooked up to wires and needles under a glass dome. Normally, the machine could detect what was inside a Poké Ball. But the professor's computer screen was filled with question marks.

"This is very puzzling," Professor Oak said. "I can't seem to open it. And I still have no idea what's inside."

"Uh, Professor Oak, what about Gary?" Ash asked. When Ash had a battle on his mind, he couldn't think of anything else.

"Oh, I'm sorry, Ash," Professor Oak said, looking up. "Gary has trekked off west to enter the Johto League."

"The Johto League?" Ash had never heard of it.

"There are a number of gyms in the western territories," Professor Oak said. "Winning a badge at eight gyms qualifies a Trainer to enter in the Johto League Championship. Gary said he's going to improve his skills by battling as many Trainers as possible."

New gyms? New Trainers? New badges? A new championship? Ash couldn't believe it.

"Well, I'm trekking west, too!" Ash said. "I'm going to enter the Johto League. We should get going right away."

"Right away?" Misty asked. "I thought we were going to take a rest."

"I'm never going to become a Pokémon Master by standing around," Ash said.

"Well, count me in," said Brock.

Professor Oak cleared his throat. "I guess that means I'll have to ask you for another favor."

The professor punched some keys on his computer. A picture of a serious-looking man with gray hair appeared on the screen.

"This is Kurt," Professor Oak said, "the famous Poké Ball designer. If anyone can figure out how to open the GS Ball, he can. He lives in the western territories."

Professor Oak handed the GS Ball to Ash.

"You want me to take it to him?" Ash asked. "No problem!"

Next, the professor handed Ash a small handheld computer. Ash had one just like it: a Pokédex. It held information on every known species of Pokémon.

"In the west, you're bound to see some brand-new Pokémon," Professor Oak explained. "This Pokédex contains information about all kinds of Pokémon you've never seen before."

"Cool," Ash said. "I can catch new Pokémon and win the Johto League Championship, too."

"And deliver the GS Ball to Kurt," Prefessor Oak reminded him. "The first stop on your journey will be New Bark Town, known as 'the town of new beginnings.'"

"New beginnings," Ash mused. "I like the sound of that. What do you think, Pikachu?"

Pikachu nodded happily. *"Pikachu!"*

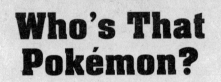

3

Who's That Pokémon?

"We'll miss you, Tracey," Ash told his friend.

"I'll miss you, too," Tracey said. "But I can't pass up the chance to stay here and study with Professor Oak."

The professor smiled. "Tracey shows great promise. I was very impressed with his sketches and reports."

Tracey's Pokémon, Marill, Venonat, and Scyther, stood next to them. Pikachu said good-bye to its friends.

Ash turned to Misty and Brock. "I guess it's the three of us again," he said. "Just like old times."

The friends left Pallet Town and began the journey west. They walked for days. To pass the time, Ash and Misty told Brock about their adventures in the Orange Islands.

One morning on their journey, Ash and the others were hiking through the woods when a thick fog rolled in. The gray clouds made it almost impossible to see ahead.

"What do we do now?" Misty asked.

"Let's keep moving," Ash said. "I think we're going in the right direction."

"I think we're going in circles," Misty complained.

"You've gotten us lost again."

"Me? You're the one who's always getting us lost," Ash snapped.

Brock stepped between them. "You two are worse than ever."

Suddenly, Togepi jumped out of Misty's arms. The tiny Pokémon quickly ran into the fog.

"*Pika!*" Pikachu ran after Togepi.

"Togepi!" Misty cried.

Ash took off after them. Luckily, he could see Pikachu's bright yellow body darting through the dense fog.

Ash ran and ran.

And then he saw it.

A blue bubble floated above the forest floor. Inside was a clear blue Pokémon.

Ash had never seen anything quite like it before. It

looked a little like a Ninetales. It stood on all fours and had a graceful body. But this Pokémon was see-through and blue, just like the bubble.

The shimmering blue bubble gently burst. The startled Pokémon jumped to the ground and sped away.

Ash's instinct was to run after it, but he was so shocked he couldn't move. He noticed Pikachu and Togepi in front of him, also transfixed by the sight of the mysterious Pokémon.

Brock and Misty ran up behind them.

"What was that?" Brock asked.

"It was so beautiful!" Misty added.

"I don't know," Ash said, coming out of his trance. "Let's find out!"

Ash ran in the direction of the Pokémon. The others followed. But the blue Pokémon was nowhere in sight.

"Now we're really lost," Misty moaned.

Just then, the thick fog lifted. They saw a town in the distance. Right in front of them was a large wooden sign.

"*Welcome to New Bark Town*," Brock read. "*The town of new beginnings*."

"All right!" Ash said happily. "My adventures in the Johto League begin here."

Ash raced into the town, talking a mile a minute. "This is going to be great. I can't wait to have my first battle. I bet there's a gym somewhere around here."

Brock grabbed him by the collar. "Slow down. First you have to register for the Johto League at the Pokémon Center."

Every town had a Pokémon Center, a place where Pokémon could be brought to rest and be healed. It was also the place for Pokémon Trainers to register for official competitions. Everywhere Ash had been so far, an orange-haired woman named Nurse Joy ran the center. They all looked alike and were all cousins.

The New Bark Town Pokémon Center was empty. When they entered, a woman's face appeared on a video screen.

"It's Nurse Joy," Misty said.

"Sorry I'm not here," Nurse Joy said. "If you need me, I'm running an errand at Professor Elm's lab." Nurse Joy went on to give directions to the lab.

"She's beautiful," Brock said dreamily. "Let's go find her!"

"Okay," Ash said. He was anxious to register for the Johto League.

The lab was just a short walk away. A police officer stood in front of the door. Ash recognized Officer Jenny – there was an Officer Jenny in every town, too.

"Hi, Officer Jenny," Ash greeted her. He started to open the door to the lab.

"Hold it right there!" she said. "You can't just walk in there. I'm conducting an investigation."

"What kind of investigation?" Ash asked.

Officer Jenny looked grim. "Someone has stolen a Pokémon from the lab!"

4

Chikorita, Cyndaquil, and Totodile

"Officer Jenny, maybe we can help," Ash suggested. "We've had some experience with stolen Pokémon."

Ash thought of Team Rocket, a trio of Pokémon thieves who were always trying to steal Pikachu. He and his friends had foiled Team Rocket's plans again and again.

"I guess it couldn't hurt," Officer Jenny said. "Come on in and I'll show you what happened."

Officer Jenny led the way into the lab. Nurse Joy was standing near a skinny man in a lab coat. The man had brown hair and glasses, and he looked very upset.

"It's all my fault," said the man. "I should have been paying attention."

"This is Professor Elm," Officer Jenny explained. "He gets new Trainers started on their Pokémon journeys."

"Just like Professor Oak in Pallet Town," Ash remarked.

Professor Elm brightened. "You know Professor Oak? He was my teacher," said the professor.

"Professor Elm," Nurse Joy scolded, "we need to concentrate on finding the stolen Pokémon."

Professor Elm nodded.

Officer Jenny pointed to a picture on a computer screen. It showed a cute, light green Pokémon with a green leaf growing from the top of its head. Ash had never seen it before.

"Each new Trainer can choose from among three Pokémon: a Grass-type, a Fire-type, and a Water-type," Officer Jenny said. "This one here is Chikorita, the Grass-type Pokémon."

"I gave the Chikorita to a young Trainer yesterday," said Professor Elm. He walked over to a steel table and picked up a Poké Ball. He opened the Poké Ball, releasing a small Pokémon.

The Pokémon had a long snout and tiny arms and legs. Its eyes looked like they were closed. There were large red spots on its back. Ash had never seen anything like it before, either.

"This is Cyndaquil, the Fire-type Pokémon," the professor said. "A Trainer is coming to pick it up tomorrow."

"How cute!" Misty said. She picked up Cyndaquil and tickled its belly.

Cyndaquil giggled. Then orange flames sprang up from Cyndaquil's back.

"Yikes!" Misty said. She placed it back on the floor.

"Don't worry, Cyndaquil won't hurt you," Professor Elm said. "It just hasn't learned to control its flames yet."

"Where's the third Pokémon, the Water-type Pokémon?" Ash asked. "Is that the one that was stolen?"

Professor Elm's face clouded. "A boy and a girl came in while I was working on an experiment. The girl said she was Nurse Joy. I let them take Totodile."

"All you had to do was look up from your experiment," Nurse Joy said. "You should be ashamed. Think how disappointed that new Trainer will be tomorrow when she can't get her Pokémon."

Ash remembered the day Professor Oak had given him Pikachu. Pikachu was his best friend. They had been through so much together. He couldn't bear to think what might have happened if someone had stolen Pikachu first.

He had to help get Totodile back.

"What does Totodile look like?" Ash asked.

Professor Elm typed something in on his computer keyboard, and Chikorita's picture disappeared. In its place was a picture of a small Pokémon that looked like a crocodile. Sharp white teeth grew in its small snout.

"What a cute Water-type Pokémon," Misty said. She loved Water-types. "I want one, too!"

"Let's figure out how to get this one back, first," Ash said.

Just then, another police officer walked in through the back of the lab. "Officer Jenny, come quickly," he said. "We found prints behind the lab."

Everyone rushed outside. Ash looked at the prints. It looked like there were two human footprints, plus the prints of some kind of Pokémon.

"I think Growlithe can help," Officer Jenny said. She threw a Poké Ball, and an orange Pokémon with black stripes on its fur and a fuzzy tail appeared. Ash knew that the police used Growlithe to solve crimes.

"I get it," Ash said. "Growlithe can sniff the prints and follow the smell straight to the criminals."

"Right," Officer Jenny replied. "Growlithe, go!"

"Pikachu, help Growlithe," Ash said.

Growlithe sniffed the footprints. Then it took off down the road, with Pikachu by its side.

Officer Jenny, Ash, Misty, and Brock followed. Growlithe and Pikachu led the way down a dirt trail and into the woods. Soon they came to a clearing.

Growlithe stopped abruptly.

"*Pika!*" Pikachu said, pointing.

"It looks like Growlithe has found Totodile," Officer Jenny replied.

Ash looked into the clearing. Officer Jenny was right. Totodile was there.

But it wasn't alone.

The little Water-type Pokémon had its sharp teeth buried in the long red hair of a girl. The girl wore a white uniform with the letter R on the front. A boy wearing the same uniform, and a white Pokémon were trying to set her free.

Ash couldn't believe it. It was Jessie, James, and Meowth — Team Rocket!

"Can't you get this thing off me?" Jessie wailed.

Officer Jenny stepped into the clearing.

"I'm placing you under arrest!" she told Team Rocket. "Release Totodile now!"

Jessie's green eyes narrowed. "Prepare to be disappointed," she said.

"Be doubly sure we're not handing it over," James added.

"We don't want to hear it," Ash said. "Just do what Officer Jenny says. A kid's going to be really upset if that Totodile isn't in the lab tomorrow. Can't you imagine how that would feel?"

"No, I really can't," James said.

"Don't you get it?" asked Meowth. "We're bad guys, remember?"

"We may be bad, but we're good at getting away," Jessie said. "Let's go!"

Jessie, James, and Meowth took off into the woods with the stolen Totodile.

"You won't get far!" Ash called out. He quickly threw a Poké Ball. "Bulbasaur, I choose you!"

A combination Grass- and Poison-type Pokémon exploded from the ball. Bulbasaur was a Seed Pokémon with a plant bulb on its back.

"Bulbasaur, Vine Whip!" Ash cried.

Two long green vines lashed out of Bulbasaur's plant bulb. The vines landed on the forest floor in front of Team Rocket. The Pokémon thieves tripped, falling face first onto the ground.

James struggled to his knees. He threw a Poké Ball.

"Weezing, go!" James cried. "Use Smoke Screen."

A purple Pokémon flew from the Poké Ball. Weezing looked like a cloud of sludge with two heads.

At James's command, thick, smelly smoke poured from Weezing's body. Ash coughed and choked as the smoke filled the clearing. Even worse, he couldn't see his opponents.

Ash had to do something fast. He reached into his belt and grabbed another Poké Ball.

"Charizard, go!" Ash yelled.

An orange-red Flame Pokémon with wings burst from the Poké Ball.

Charizard breathed fiery sparks into the air and stomped its thick legs on the ground.

"Charizard, get rid of this Smoke Screen!" Ash yelled.

Charizard flapped its big wings. The breeze quickly cleared the smoke from Weezing's attack.

Bulbasaur saw its chance. It lashed out with its Vine Whip, slicing through Jessie's hair just above the point where Totodile was hanging on.

"*Ouch!*" Jessie cried as Totodile landed on the ground. Ash scooped up the little Water-type Pokémon and ran away from Jessie.

"Nice work, Bulbasaur," Ash told his Pokémon.

"Thank goodness," Jessie said. "That toothsome Totodile finally let go of me."

Meowth kicked Jessie's boot in frustration. "You let

it get away!" said the Pokémon.

James bopped Meowth on the head. "I didn't see you do anything to stop it."

"Hey, watch the fur!" Meowth said.

Team Rocket's argument erupted into a fistfight. Jessie, James, and Meowth pinched, kicked, and slapped one another silly.

Totodile ran up and faced Team Rocket. The little Water-type Pokémon hit them with a fierce water blast. Pikachu, Charizard, and Bulbasaur all joined Totodile in the attack.

Jessie, James, and Meowth flew off into the sky.

"Looks like Team Rocket's blasting off again!" they cried.

Ash handed Officer Jenny the Totodile. "Here you go."

Officer Jenny smiled at the Pokémon. "You'll make a new Trainer very happy."

"I know," Ash said. "And now I can register for the Johto League!"

5

The Forest of the Heracross

Ash and his friends went back to the Pokémon Center. Nurse Joy was waiting for them.

"I just need your Pokédex, Ash," she said.

Nurse Joy walked to a machine in the corner of the lobby. It looked like a computer with a large screen. Nurse Joy slipped Ash's Pokédex into a slot on the keyboard. Ash's picture appeared on the screen. The letters OK flashed next to his picture.

Nurse Joy handed the Pokédex back to Ash. "Now you're all signed up. You need to earn eight badges if you want to compete in the championship." She handed Ash a small book. "This is your guidebook to the Johto League gyms. Don't lose it!"

"I won't," Ash said. "So, where should I start?"

"The closest gym is the Violet Gym in Violet City," Nurse Joy said. "It's a few days' journey from here."

"A few days?" Misty moaned.

"No problem," Ash said. "I can't wait to get my first badge!" Ash grabbed his friends and ran out of the Pokémon Center.

Over the next few days, Ash, Misty, and Brock talked about what they had seen in New Bark Town.

"It's sort of like Pallet Town, but different," Ash was saying as they walked through a lush forest. "Trainers in Pallet Town get to choose from Bulbasaur, Charmander, or Squirtle. In New Bark Town, they get to choose from Chikorita, Cyndaquil, or Totodile."

"I wonder if Pokémon Trainers who sleep late still get a Pikachu," Misty teased. Ash had started out with a Pikachu because he overslept, and there were no other Pokémon left by the time he got to Professor Oak's lab.

Ash blushed. "I just think it's cool, that's all."

"I'd probably choose a Cyndaquil if I were a new Trainer," Brock said. "It has some amazing fire power."

Suddenly, Misty stopped. "Hey, guys. Does this forest look weird to you?"

Ash looked around. The trees they had just seen were full and leafy. But the trees here were stripped of all their leaves. They looked brown and lifeless.

"It looks like something is eating the trees," Brock said.

"Pika!" Pikachu said, startled. It pointed to a nearby tree.

"What's the matter, Pikachu?" Ash asked.

They moved closer to the tree. Ash could make out something climbing on the tree trunk.

"It's a big Bug- and Fighting-type Pokémon!" Misty cried. "That tree is crawling with them!" She shivered. Ash knew that Misty hated Bug-type Pokémon, even though she loved all kinds of weird-looking Water-type Pokémon.

The Bug- and Fighting-type Pokémon were grayish-black, with round bodies, antennae, and horns on their foreheads that forked at the end. Ash noticed that they were pretty big for Bug-type Pokémon — a little taller than him.

Ash took out his Pokédex to get more information.

"Heracross, a Single Horn Pokémon," Dexter said. "Though good-natured, it is very powerful and uses its horn to flip opponents upside down. It loves the sweet sap that drips from trees."

"Good-natured and powerful!" Ash said. "I could use a Pokémon like that. I'm gonna catch one."

Ash took an empty Poké Ball from his belt and started to throw it at a Heracross.

"Hold it right there!" a deep voice cried.

Ash froze. A tall, bearded man wearing a red jumpsuit, boots, and a round hat stepped up to them.

The man extended a hand. "I'm Woodruff, a ranger for the forest service," he said.

Ash, Brock, and Misty introduced themselves.

"Am I doing something wrong?" Ash asked. "It's okay for Pokémon Trainers to catch wild Pokémon, isn't it?"

"Of course," Woodruff said. "But you might want to think about the effect it will have on the environment. This forest is an especially well-balanced habitat. The Heracross here live a peaceful life. You might disturb that balance."

"*Those* Heracross?" Ash asked. The big Single Horn Pokémon didn't look peaceful to him.

Just then, Butterfree, a Bug- and Flying-type Pokémon, flew up and landed next to the Heracross on the tree. The Butterfree and Heracross ate sap side by side.

"See how calm they are?" Woodruff pointed out.

"Heracross even lets Butterfree feed right next to it, without bothering it at all."

"That *is* peaceful," Brock agreed.

Misty didn't look convinced. "If this forest is so peaceful and balanced, then why are all the trees eaten up?"

Woodruff's face clouded. "A species of Pokémon has invaded the forest. They're disturbing the balance."

"What kind of Pokémon would do that?" Brock asked.

"*Pika! Pika!*" Pikachu pointed again.

Ash saw a strange brown mass moving along the forest floor toward the Heracross and Butterfree. Shocked, Ash realized that it was a swarm of Bug-type Pokémon.

These Pokémon had round bodies, like the Heracross. But they each had a mouth filled with sharp teeth and two pointed claws above their eyes.

Ash recognized them. "Pinsir!" he cried. "They're going to attack the Heracross!"

6

Pinsir Attack!

The Pinsir climbed up the tree trunk. They clicked their sharp claws.

Startled, the Butterfree flew away.

"Hey, all you Heracross!" Misty called out. "Do something! Stop those Pinsir!"

The Heracross heard Misty. Transparent wings spread out on their backs. The Heracross flew off the tree trunk, then flew back again, aimed right for the Pinsir.

The Pinsir didn't back down. They clicked their claws at the Heracross.

The Heracross stopped in midair, afraid. Then they

turned around and flew to another tree.

"Those Heracross look pretty tough," Misty said. "But I guess they're not as strong as they look."

"Actually, the Heracross could defeat the Pinsir if they wanted to," Woodruff explained, "but they're too gentle by nature."

"That's just what Dexter said," Ash remarked. "Good-natured and powerful."

Brock was carefully studying the trees. "I think I see what's happening. The Pinsir chased off the Heracross. Then the Heracross had to suck sap from trees they've already eaten from. That makes the trees dry up."

"That's right," Woodruff said. "There's plenty of sap for Heracross and Butterfree in this part of the forest. But there's not enough for Pinsir, too."

"Hey, look!" Ash interrupted them. "That Butterfree's in trouble."

A Butterfree was stuck in a crook in the tree, surrounded by a group of angry Pinsir. A Heracross flew between the Butterfree and the Pinsir.

"What a brave Heracross," Brock said. "It's protecting that Butterfree!"

The Heracross tried to drive the Pinsir away with its horn. But there were just too many of them.

Ash didn't think that was fair. "Pinsir, you can't gang up on one Pokémon," he said. "Bulbasaur, I choose you!"

Ash threw a Poké Ball, and Bulbasaur appeared.

"Bulbasaur, Vine Whip!" Ash yelled.

The strong vines sprung from Bulbasaur's bulb and lashed at the attacking Pinsir. One by one, the Pinsir fell to the grass. The Butterfree quickly flew away.

But the Heracross couldn't move.

"It's too weak," Brock observed.

The group of Pinsir got back on their feet and climbed up the tree trunk.

Ash knew he needed more help.

"Pikachu, Thundershock!" he cried.

Electricity sparked from Pikachu's red cheeks as the Electric-type Pokémon charged up for the attack. Then Pikachu let loose with a white-hot blast.

The blast shocked the Pinsir, sending them falling back to the ground. But the Pinsir were tough. They jumped back to their feet and ran up the tree again.

"Pikachu, Thunder!" Ash yelled.

"Pikaaaaaaaaaaa!" Pikachu hit them with another electric charge, this one bigger than before.

The group of Pinsir fell to the ground one more time. This time, they were too frazzled to get up. They skittled along the ground, away from Pikachu and Heracross.

Safe at last, Heracross flew down from the tree. It landed on Bulbasaur's plant bulb and tried to suck sap from it.

Bulbasaur knocked it off with one of its vines.

Ash laughed. "I guess Heracross are crazy for sap!" He turned to Pikachu. "Good work, Pikachu. You scared off those Pinsir."

"It's not that simple," Woodruff said. "Those Pinsir will be back."

"What do you mean?" Misty asked.

"The Heracross and Pinsir used to live in separate territories. But lately, the Pinsir have been invading the Heracross territory," Woodruff said. "Something must have disturbed the Pinsir, and I'm going to find out what it is."

"We can help," Ash said. He couldn't stand to think of the Pinsir attacking the Heracross and Butterfree again.

Woodruff nodded. "I could use some extra hands. Follow me."

"Oh, great," Misty muttered. "Just what I always wanted to do. Go off on a search for bugs. Yuck!"

The forest ranger led them off the main forest trail

into a heavily wooded area. "The bush around here is incredibly thick," Woodruff said. "It'll be slow going."

"Leave it to me," Ash said. "Bulbasaur, Razor Leaf!"

Sharp-edged leaves flew from Bulbasaur's plant bulb. They sliced through the vines and branches ahead, clearing a path.

Brock looked behind them as they walked. "Hey, that Heracross is following us," he said.

Ash looked back. The Single Horn Pokémon was walking along with a smile on its face.

"Maybe it thinks it owes us for helping it back there," he said.

"Or maybe it wants another sip from Bulbasaur's plant bulb!" said Misty.

Soon the trees thinned out, and they didn't need Bulbasaur's Razor Leaf anymore. Ash called the Pokémon safely back into its Poké Ball.

"Here we are," Woodruff said.

Ash saw, with amazement, that they had walked up to the edge of a deep canyon. He carefully looked over the side. There was a long, long drop into a river below. He guessed that the canyon was about ten or twenty feet wide. It looked impossible to cross.

"This canyon divides the Heracross territory from the Pinsir territory," Woodruff said.

"I can see that," Ash said. "How are we supposed to get to the other side?"

"No problem," the forest ranger replied. "There's a rope bridge a little farther along."

Ash and the others followed Woodruff along the canyon. Soon they came to the bridge.

It was hanging limply over the side of the canyon. The ropes holding up the bridge had been slashed!

"Did the Pinsir do this, too?" Misty asked.

Woodruff held up a piece of rope.

"This was cut by humans," he said. "Somebody doesn't want us to get into the Pinsir forest."

"What do we do now?" Ash asked.

Misty pointed to Heracross. The Single Horn Pokémon was eating sap from a nearby tree.

"Heracross doesn't seem worried. It's having a snack," she said.

"I think it's doing more than that," Brock said. "Look!"

The tree that Heracross was eating from grew weak and wobbly. It toppled over with a crash, landing on the other side of the canyon.

"That Heracross built a bridge for us!" Ash said. He and Pikachu started to walk across the tree.

"That's not a bridge," Misty said. "That's an old tree. No way am I walking across that thing!"

But Misty didn't have a choice. Togepi jumped out of her arms and toddled across the tree trunk. "Togepi," she cried, "come back!" Misty got on all fours and crawled after the baby Spike Ball Pokémon. She grabbed it and then continued across the bridge. Woodruff, Brock, and Heracross followed.

Once they were across, Woodruff led the way again. They walked along a trail.

"We're almost at the Pinsir forest," he said. "Be careful, everyone."

Ash gasped. The trees in the Pinsir forest were just as bare and lifeless as the trees in the Heracross forest.

"Something strange is going on here," Brock said.

Pikachu tugged on Ash's jeans. *Pika! Pikachu!*

Ash saw what Pikachu was so excited about. A large Pinsir was sucking sap from a nearby tree. The

Pinsir looked shiny, like it was made of metal. And its movements were stiff.

"What's that thing over there?" Ash asked the others.

"Isn't it a Pinsir?" Misty asked.

A look of shock crossed Woodruff's face. "It's a mechanical Pinsir," he cried. "A robot!"

7

Heracross vs. the Pinsir Robot

"Who in the world would create a Pinsir robot?" Ash wondered.

"A team of geniuses, of course," said a voice.

Jessie, James, and Meowth jumped out from behind a tree.

"Team Rocket!" Ash cried. "But why?"

"This twerp is twerpier than I thought," Jessie said. "To get rich. Why else?"

"The sap from these trees is supersweet," James said. "Once we bottle it and sell it to tourists, we'll be rolling in money. And there's nothing sweeter than that!"

Meowth grinned. "And we don't even have to do the work. This buggy pile of nuts and bolts is doing it all for us."

Meowth was right. The sap the Pinsir was collecting from the tree traveled directly from the robot's body into two large rocket-shaped tanks on its back.

"See? No fuss, no mess," Jessie said. "Until you troublemakers showed up."

"You're the troublemakers," Ash said. "Your Pinsir robot is driving the real Pinsir away from the forest. Now they're invading Heracross territory."

Woodruff sadly nodded his head. "It's destroying the balance of nature."

"Forget the balance of nature," Jessie sneered. "We're trying to balance our budget here."

Jessie and James each threw out a Poké Ball.

"Go, Lickitung!" Jessie cried.

"Go, Victreebel!" yelled James.

Lickitung immediately began slurping sap from the tree with its long tongue. Victreebel ate the sap, too.

"Hey!" James said, surprised. "You're supposed to attack!"

Meowth picked up a small remote control.

"This Pinsir was designed for collecting sap, but it's pretty good in battle, too," Meowth said. "Go, robotic Pinsir!"

The mechanical Pinsir climbed down from the tree and faced Ash and his friends. Victreebel and Lickitung kept eating the delicious sap, too busy to battle.

Ash threw out Bulbasaur's Poké Ball. "Bulbasaur, Razor Leaf!" he yelled.

Dozens of sharp leaves flew out of Bulbasaur's plant bulb, hitting the robot Pinsir. The Pinsir deflected the leaves with its strong metal claws.

Meowth smiled proudly. "Razor Leaf can't harm its metal body."

Ash didn't give up. "Bulbasaur, Vine Whip!"

Bulbasaur wrapped the robotic Pinsir in its strong

vines, then spun the mechanical Pokémon around and around like a top. The attack left Pinsir weak and dizzy.

"Now, Pikachu," Ash called out. "Thundershock!"

Pikachu focused all its energy on the attack. It hurled a powerful electric blast at the robotic Pinsir.

The Pinsir's body glowed with electricity. It seemed to absorb the charge.

Meowth grinned. "This Pinsir is programmed to absorb Electric attacks and then release them against its opponent."

Meowth pulled a lever on the remote control. "This is revenge for all those times Pikachu sent us blasting off!" it said.

Pinsir's eyes burned with an eerie blue light. A lightning bolt shot out from the mechanical Pinsir, zapping Ash, Misty, Brock, Woodruff, Pikachu, and Bulbasaur.

Ash's body tingled with the charge. He tried to run away, but the electricity had him frozen to the spot.

"I can't move!" he cried.

None of the others could move, either.

Meowth hit another button. "Go get 'em, Pinsir!"

The robotic Pinsir marched toward Ash and his friends. Its metal claws clicked menacingly. The electric current still flowed from its body, holding Ash and the others in place.

"It's coming this way!" Misty cried.

Ash closed his eyes. He couldn't bear to watch. Then he heard a familiar voice.

"*He-Ra-Cross!*"

The Bug- and Fighting-type Pokémon ran in front of the mechanical Pinsir. It pushed against the robot, keeping it away from Ash and the others.

Meowth laughed. "Does this Heracross think it can stop my mechanical masterpiece?" it said.

The robotic Pinsir charged at Heracross. Heracross used its horn to keep the robot's claws at bay. It pushed against the Pinsir with all its might. Sweat dripped down its body.

"Hang in there, Heracross!" Ash called out.

Heracross pushed and pushed. Then it thrust forward one more time, slowly pushing the robotic Pinsir backward.

Ash saw the blue glow in Pinsir's eyes grow dim. The electric current had stopped.

They were free! Ash quickly ran behind Pinsir and grabbed one of the tanks of sap from its back. Brock grabbed the other.

Meowth frantically hit buttons on the remote control.

But the mechanical Pinsir was helpless against the amazing strength of Heracross.

"We've got to do something before they get away with our sap," Jessie said.

James ran over and grabbed the remote. "Give me that!" he cried. "I'll fix things."

Jessie tried to grab the remote from him. "Leave it to me," she said.

"Hey, I'm the robot expert here!" Meowth protested.

While Team Rocket struggled with the remote, Heracross made its final move. It lifted up the robot, then threw it high into the air.

The robotic Pinsir landed right next to Team Rocket! The force sent Jessie, James, and Meowth flying into the air.

"Looks like we're blasting off again!" they cried.

Ash ran over and hugged Heracross. "You did it, Heracross!"

"Heracross!" said the Bug-type Pokémon happily. It smiled at Ash.

Ash, Misty, and Brock spent the rest of the afternoon helping Woodruff clean up the forest. Soon the Pinsir were back in their territory, and the Heracross and Butterfree were no longer afraid.

"Thanks for your help," Woodruff told them.

Ash and his friends said good-bye to Woodruff. Then they headed back down the trail toward the next town. They had walked along for a while when Pikachu suddenly stopped and turned around.

"Pika!" said the yellow Pokémon, pointing at a friendly figure behind them. It was Heracross! The Single Horn Pokémon was still following them.

"Go on back to your friends, Heracross," Misty told it kindly.

Heracross shook its head.

"Do you want to come along with us?" Ash asked it.

Heracross smiled and nodded.

Ash threw a Poké Ball toward Heracross. The Poké Ball opened, red light beamed out, and Heracross disappeared inside the ball.

Ash proudly held up the Poké Ball.

"I did it!" he shouted. "I caught a Heracross!"

The Valley of the Donphan

Heracross joined Ash and the others as they continued on their journey. Ash spent the next few days getting to know his new Pokémon. But he hadn't forgotten about the Johto League. "According to this, we're just a few miles away from Violet City and the Violet Gym," Ash said. He had his face buried in a map.

"Does that map say anything about this valley?" Misty asked him.

"Huh?" Ash folded the map. They had come to the edge of a cliff. The cliff's rocky slopes led into a valley bordered by mountains on each side.

"We have to cross it to get to Violet City," Brock said.

"There's no mountain high enough and no valley low enough to stop a future Pokémon Master like me!" Ash said with determination.

Ash and his friends carefully made their way down into the valley. Rocks rolled under their feet as they struggled to keep their balance. But soon they reached the bottom.

Ash scanned the valley. Lush trees and bushes dotted areas with blankets of dark green. Big rocks jutted out in other areas.

A large Pokémon walked out from behind one of the trees. The dark gray creature looked tough. It walked on all fours and had a long trunk that looked like it was made of armor. The armor covered the Pokémon's back, too. Two curved white tusks protruded from either side of its trunk.

"What is it?" Ash wondered. He flipped open Dexter, his Pokédex.

"Donphan," Dexter said. A picture of the strange Pokémon appeared on Dexter's screen. "With its hard, sharp tusks and even more durable skin, Donphan is able to knock down buildings with its Tackle attack. Donphan's tusks grow longer as it gains experience."

"Hey, Ash," Brock said. "Didn't you meet a Trainer once who had this Pokémon?"

"Yeah, you're right," Ash said. "It was really powerful. I'm going to catch it." He reached for a Poké Ball.

Brock held out a hand to stop him. "Hold on, Ash," he said. "That Donphan's tusks are much shorter than the picture in your Pokédex. It's obviously in need of a good Pokémon breeder. I should catch it."

"But I found it," Ash protested.

"We all found it together," Brock replied.

Misty rolled her eyes. "While you two are arguing, the Donphan is getting away."

"Not if I can help it," Brock said. He quickly threw out a Poké Ball. "Go, Onix!"

A huge Rock Snake Pokémon appeared in a blaze of light.

"Onix, Tackle!" Brock called out.

Onix slammed its huge body into the ground, blocking Donphan's path. The ground trembled.

Donphan flew up, then landed squarely on its feet.

The Pokémon jumped into the air and curled its body into a ball. It rolled across the ground, aiming right for Onix.

Onix lifted its head, ready to deliver another tackle. It didn't have a chance. Donphan crashed into Onix. The Rock- and Ground-type Pokémon reeled from the mighty blow. Onix slammed to the ground and fainted.

Brock looked shocked. "Onix, return!" he called out. He shook his head. "That little thing is strong."

"Let me try it," Ash said. He threw out a Poké Ball. "Heracross, I choose you!"

Heracross popped out of the Poké Ball, ready to battle.

"Heracross, Tackle!" Ash yelled.

Heracross charged after Donphan, ramming into it with the strong horn on top of its head. Donphan fell to the ground.

Donphan wasn't knocked out, though. It quickly got to its feet and rolled into a ball once again. Then it zoomed toward Heracross.

The Bug- and Fighting-type Pokémon was ready. Heracross lowered its horn. It batted Donphan away with a powerful swing. Donphan crashed into a nearby tree.

"Great, Heracross!" Ash said proudly. "One more move should do it."

"Hey! Stop that!" a voice cried.

A girl about Brock's age ran next to the Donphan. She had short black hair and wore a purple dress. She hugged Donphan. "Are you hurt?" she asked it.

"Is this your Pokémon?" Ash asked her. "I thought it was wild."

"I'm its Trainer," she said. "I let all my Donphan run free in this valley."

"I'm sorry," Ash said. "I didn't know."

Brock rushed up to the girl. He shook her hand. "I tried to stop him. I really did. I'm Brock."

Ash groaned. Brock would say or do anything to make a good impression on a girl.

"I'm Rochelle," the girl replied.

Ash saw that Rochelle wore a smooth, brown stone speckled with gold on a cord around her neck.

Brock noticed it, too. "That's a beautiful necklace," he said.

"It's agate," Rochelle said. "The stone is prized for its rich colors. It used to be worn by kings and queens. My Donphan are trained to search for the stone in this valley."

"They're pretty amazing Pokémon," Ash said.

"I know," said Rochelle. "We'd better get going. Don't go battling any more Donphan while you're here, okay?"

Ash nodded. "Sure."

From behind a rock, three Pokémon thieves watched Rochelle and Donphan walk away.

They were Jessie, James, and Meowth, of course. Team Rocket was up to no good once again.

"Did you hear what she said?" Jessie asked.

"Loud and clear," James replied. "If we capture that Donphan, it will lead us to the agate."

Meowth got a dreamy look in its eyes. "Agate, the stone of kings and queens," it said. "If we get enough agate, we can buy our own castle and live happily ever after!"

"First we have to get Donphan," James reminded him.

"No problem," Meowth said. The Scratch Cat Pokémon reached behind a rock and pulled out a long tube. Meowth handed it to Jessie. Then it pressed a button on a remote control, and Team Rocket's balloon appeared in the air above them. A rope ladder dropped down from the balloon basket. James and Meowth hopped onto the ladder.

"Let's get this Donphan plan over and done with!" Meowth cried.

"Right!" Jessie said. She jumped up on the rock. Rochelle and Donphan were right below.

"You're done for, Donphan!" Jessie yelled. Then she pressed a button on the tube, and a net shot out, covering Donphan.

The balloon flew low right over Donphan. James and Meowth reached down and attached the net to the bottom of the balloon. Jessie climbed up the rope ladder.

"We've done it!" James cried. "Donphan is ours!"

Save Donphan!

"Donphan!" Rochelle called out. "Where are you?"

Ash heard Rochelle's cry. "Something's wrong. Let's go help her," he said.

"I'm way ahead of you," said Brock, running past Ash.

Soon Ash, Misty, and Brock found Rochelle. She looked upset.

"Did you see two people in white uniforms?" she asked. "They took my Donphan. They had a talking Meowth with them, too."

"Team Rocket!" Ash, Misty, and Brock said together. Then they told Rochelle all about the Pokémon thieves.

"We'll help you find Donphan," Brock said. He threw a Poké Ball. Out came Zubat, a purple-and-blue Bat Pokémon.

"Zubat can use Supersonic to sense objects far away," Brock said. "Zubat, find Team Rocket!"

Zubat flew high into the sky. The Pokémon flew in a circle around them. Then it landed on Brock's shoulder.

"There are too many rocks and trees in the way," Brock said. "They're blocking Zubat's Supersonic."

"I have an idea," Rochelle said. She took out a silver whistle from a pocket in her dress. Then she blew on the whistle, letting out a long, high-pitched tone.

Ash wondered what Rochelle was doing.

Four Donphan came running through the trees toward Rochelle. They lined up in a row in front of her.

"Good job," Rochelle said. "That was fast!"

"Are these all yours, Rochelle?" Misty asked her.

Rochelle nodded.

"You did a great job raising them," Brock said. "Their tusks are all so well developed."

Rochelle frowned. "I'm worried. Those villains captured the youngest Donphan," she said. She turned to the rest of the Donphan. "Okay, everyone. Let's find our missing friend."

Ash watched as the four Donphan sniffed the ground with their long trunks. They weaved in and out of rocks, trees, and bushes. They all seemed to be headed in the same direction.

"They must be onto something," Misty remarked.

Soon the Donphan led them to a rocky area dotted with only a few trees. Jessie, James, and Meowth were sitting in the dirt, exhausted. The stolen Donphan sniffed at the rocks nearby.

Ash stepped forward. "What are you doing with that Donphan?" he asked.

Jessie stood up. "Prepare for trouble . . ." she said.

"...and make it – oh, forget it," James said. "I'm too pooped."

"We've been following this Donphan all over the valley," Meowth complained, "and we still haven't found any agate."

"You mean, that's why you stole the Donphan?" Misty asked. "You wanted to use it to find agate?"

Jessie nodded. "That's right. But so far, this Donphan is a dud."

"That poor little Donphan is too young to find agate," Rochelle said.

"That Donphan belongs to Rochelle," Ash said. "Give it back!"

Jessie and James looked at each other. "Team Rocket? Give back a Pokémon?"

"We stole it fair and square," Meowth added.

Jessie and James each threw a Poké Ball. White light flashed, and Victreebel and Arbok appeared.

Victreebel swallowed James in one gulp.

James's legs kicked and he tried to squirm out. "Don't attack me!" James shouted.

Victreebel spit out James and turned on Ash and the others.

"Don't worry, Rochelle!" Brock yelled. "I'll protect you. Go, Onix!"

The large Rock- and Ground-type Pokémon exploded from its Poké Ball.

"Onix, Bind!" Brock called out.

Onix wrapped its large body around Victreebel, squeezing the Pokémon in a rocky grip.

"Victreebel, Sleep Powder!" James commanded.

Shimmering golden powder sprinkled out of Victreebel's mouth and covered Onix's head. The Rock Snake Pokémon collapsed to the ground, sound asleep.

"No!" Brock cried.

Ash and Misty exchanged glances. "Looks like we're up next," Misty said.

Both Trainers threw Poké Balls into the air.

"Heracross, I choose you!" Ash yelled, and the Bug- and Fighting-type Pokémon flashed into the valley.

"Poliwag, go!" Misty cried. A round purple Pokémon hopped out of the ball. Poliwag had two squat legs, two big eyes, and a long, flat tail. The Water-type Pokémon had a white belly marked with a black spiral pattern.

Jessie didn't look worried. "This is just perfect," she said. "Not only do we get a Donphan, we'll get all of your Pokémon, too."

"Not if I can help it," Misty said. "Poliwag, Doubleslap!"

Poliwag hopped over to Victreebel and began fiercely slapping the Pokémon with its strong tail. Victreebel's yellow flower bell turned red from the blows.

"Now follow up with Bubble attack!" Misty yelled.

A strong stream of bubbles poured from Poliwag's

mouth. The bubbles sent Victreebel reeling backward. Victreebel's open mouth landed right on James's head. James tipped over and landed on top of Meowth.

"Not again!" James moaned.

"*Meowth!* I'm getting squished!" complained the Pokémon.

Now Jessie's Pokémon was ready for action. "*Arbok!*" hissed the Cobra Pokémon.

"Heracross, Tackle!" Ash shouted.

Arbok flew at Heracross. Heracross ran forward and slammed into Arbok with all its might.

The attack knocked Arbok into Jessie. They both crashed into James, Meowth, and Victreebel. Team Rocket and their Pokémon lay in a heap on the ground.

Ash saw his chance. "Heracross, Horn attack!"

Heracross lowered its shiny black horn. The Pokémon raced forward, then jabbed Team Rocket.

Team Rocket flew into the air, landing in their balloon basket.

Then Pikachu stepped up. The Electric-type Pokémon let loose with a Thundershock attack. The balloon – and everyone inside it – sizzled from the electric charge.

One of Pikachu's lightning bolts ripped into the balloon.

"The balloon's got a hole!" Jessie wailed.

James sighed. "Our plans always have holes in them."

The burst balloon spiraled across the sky.

"Looks like Team Rocket's blasting off again!" Team Rocket yelled as they disappeared over the horizon.

10

A Battle of Skill

Rochelle hugged her young Donphan. "I'm so glad you're safe," she said. She turned to Ash and the others. "I owe this one to you guys. I wish there was some way I could thank you."

"Maybe there is," Ash said. "I'd really love the chance to battle one of your Donphan."

"That's Ash for you," Misty said. "He's got battles on the brain."

"If I'm going to become a Pokémon Master, I need to get all the experience I can," Ash said. He turned to Rochelle. "What do you say? Are your Pokémon ready?"

"No problem," Rochelle said.

"All right!" Ash cheered. Battling a Donphan would be great training for him and his Pokémon. He looked over the group of Donphan. "I choose that one with the big tusks."

"Fine." Rochelle motioned to the Donphan and walked about twenty paces away. Then they turned and faced Ash.

Ash knew exactly what strategy he would use. He looked over at Heracross, still triumphant from helping to defeat Team Rocket. "Heracross, I choose you!"

"*Heracross!*" The Single Horn Pokémon stood at Ash's side, ready to battle.

Rochelle made the first move. "Donphan, Tackle!"

Donphan snorted and charged at Heracross, its powerful legs moving at great speed.

"Heracross, Endure!" Ash called out.

Heracross leaned over and stopped Donphan's attack with its horn.

"Now give it a toss!" Ash yelled.

Heracross picked up Donphan. The Bug- and Fighting-type Pokémon threw Donphan, and the Pokémon landed on its feet.

"Good job, Donphan," Rochelle said. "Now, show them your Roll Out attack!"

Donphan moved quickly. It curled up into a ball, and then rolled across the ground like a wheel.

Heracross dodged the speeding Pokémon. It turned and looked at Ash, pleased.

"Heracross, behind you!" Ash warned.

It was too late. Donphan rolled back to Heracross. It slammed into Heracross, sending the Single Horn Pokémon flying. Heracross landed in a nearby tree.

Immediately, Heracross started sucking sap from

the tree trunk.

"Hey!" Ash cried. "This is no time for sap sucking!"

"Maybe it needs the sap for energy," Brock guessed.

Heracross finished its snack and flew off the tree. It faced Donphan once again.

"Donphan, Tackle again!" Rochelle called out.

Donphan charged after Heracross.

"Heracross, Horn attack!" Ash countered.

The Bug-type Pokémon picked up Donphan and tossed it into the air.

"Donphan, turn that into Roll Out attack," Rochelle said.

As Donphan hit the ground, it immediately curled up its body into the shape of a wheel. It used the momentum from Heracross's toss to build up speed.

Heracross tried to dodge the attacking Donphan, but the Pokémon was unstoppable. Donphan slammed into Heracross with incredible force. The Bug- and Fighting-type Pokémon went down with a thud.

Ash rushed to his Pokémon's side. "Heracross? Are you okay?"

"*Hera . . .*" replied the Pokémon weakly.

It couldn't get up.

"It looks like Donphan wins this battle," Rochelle said. She walked over and shook Ash's hand.

"That Donphan is strong," Ash said.

"And your Heracross really shows promise," Rochelle said. "I'm sure you'll do a great job training it."

"I hope you're not too disappointed, Ash," Misty said.

Ash thought about it.

Since he began his journey out west, he had seen a Cyndaquil, a cool new Fire-type Pokémon, and Chikorita, a Grass-type Pokémon. He had rescued a Totodile. He had caught a Heracross. He had even battled a Donphan.

"Disappointed?" Ash said. "No way! I can't wait to see what else is waiting for us out here in the wild west!"

About the Author

Tracey West has been writing books for more than twenty years. She enjoys watching cartoons, reading comic books, and taking long walks in the woods (looking for wild Pokémon). She lives in a small town in New York with her family and pets.